Ben
and
the
Dragon

Illustrated
by Andrée Weimer

David W. Weimer

One and Only Press

Ben and the Dragon

First Edition: 2013

Printed in the United States of America

Fonts: Garamond

Main entry under title: Ben and the Dragon

1. Children's Fiction 2. Fantasy

ISBN: 978-0-9850578-1-7

Visit the author's website:

www.oneandonlyobserver.wordpress.com

Merry Christmas, Ben.

Table of Contents

Chapter 1 – Surprise

Flushing, Ohio, December

One early winter day, a boy named Ben saw a dragon in the water.

He was at the pond's edge, watching the minnows hover, dart and stir up tan clouds with their tails, swishing sediment and pebbles in the shallow water. While counting the fish, he noticed out of the corner of his eye a large shape drifting from the right. It stopped in front of him in the water. It was a bright day with no clouds.

7

Ben thought it was his brother. He continued to count the tiny fish.

"There are nine in one spot here, Gui," he said. "Quick, look for a container."

There was no reply.

It surprised Ben that his brother had arrived so silently. Normally, he always heard him coming. Now, he wasn't speaking.

"Come on, Gui! They're all swimming in one place. I need something to scoop with!"

"What is a container?" a deep voice rumbled.

The eight-year-old's heart lurched with a jolt of fear. He scrambled to his feet and looked behind him—no one!

Up the hill, he saw Gui and Mom swinging. Dad was walking their dog Mike on the gravel drive.

Uh oh…

Ben turned slowly to look back at the water. The shadow was still there. He looked up at the sky. No clouds. There was no overhanging tree here, either, only a *No Swimming* sign nearby. The shadow drifted closer and the boy's hoped-for guess faded. It wasn't the sign's shadow.

The sun sparkled from a multitude of shifting places within the darkness on the surface. Without substance, it didn't seem like anything he recognized except… well, a shadow.

Ben searched the water near his feet for the minnows. They were gone.

"I don't need a container anymore," he whispered to himself.

"Yes. I regret that I frightened them away." The voice coming from the shadow vibrated the air like a far-away fog horn.

Ben swallowed. "What *are* you? Are you *real?*"

"Our worlds are close to one another at this time of night and light."

The boy shook his head. "It's not night."

"It is always 'night' on my world," the shadow replied.

Ben felt another spike of fear in his belly. Yet he was curious. It didn't seem possible he could be talking to a shadow.

"What are you?" he asked again.

"Your kind calls ours dra-guon."

"Drag-oon?"

"Your species considers mine a myth."

Something clicked in Ben's mind…. "You mean— you breathe fire, and fly, and eat people and steal treasure? You're a water dragon!"

The rumbling voice chuckled. Two faceted crystalline eyes appeared in the upper part of the shadow. They sparkled a friendly green and gradually shifted to turquoise.

"To 'steal' is against our nature. And we don't 'eat' people—although certain… elements in your world are reported to be fabulous."

Ben was thrilled to know he was talking to an actual water dragon.

"How do you breathe fire under water?" he asked.

"My image exists on the reflection. I am not under the 'water' before you. Our two worlds reside, temporarily, in the *Temps-rapproché*, a 'close-time.' I see you in my *l'eau* pool as you perceive me in yours.

"But you're in the *water!*" the eight-year-old persisted.

"Are you?" the dragon rumbled.

Ben wanted to ask his second question, or his second group of questions. "No, but how do you fly? And what do you look like? Can you really see *me* from another world?"

Within the shadow, a previously vague shape with glowing eyes grew distinct. Ben saw large wings unfold and spread wide. Four limbs separated from a central mass and a long serpentine neck curved up to a teeth-studded jaw on a narrow, regal head.

It looks exactly like a dragon, Ben thought.

But this one seemed to be made of blue rock candy —all sharp edges, facets and shifting color.

The shadow dragon's scales appeared to be glass or crystal. Its wings folded, and the dragon posed exactly like a picture from the book he was reading for school.

The pond's surface rippled suddenly with a breeze and the dragon's image faded into shadow. It reappeared after the water was still again.

"Is that really what you look like?" Ben asked.

The dragon nodded. Its body shimmered liquid green, matching the color of its cat-like emerald eyes.

The boy was temporarily out of questions. He looked back again and saw his dad walking another lap on the path around the playground. Gui and Mom were talking and laughing while swinging.

Ben looked back down at the dragon and sighed. "I wish I could be you."

"Indeed," the dragon replied, its eyes shifting to cobalt blue, "you *may*."

Ben's toes squished in the grass and mud at the pond's edge. He backed up and squatted. "What do you mean?"

The dragon spoke without moving its jaws. It stared at him and Ben heard its deep rumbling voice. He wondered if he was imagining everything.

"Over thousands of your human years, on rare occasions, some of you have translated here and returned again to your world; this is the source of your legends.

"When our two kinds meet at this boundary during a 'close-time,' they have the possibility of exchanging places briefly."

Ben didn't understand, and said so. The dragon in the water explained that when they touched the boundary between their worlds at the same time—the water—they would exchange places!

This felt to Ben like he was standing at the coping, on the top edge of a half-pipe with his skates on at the concrete bowl park in Wheeling—scared, but *wanting* to try.

"I'm scared," he said.

"As am I," the dragon replied.

"Well…" Ben stood. "I think I'll go play with Mom and Gui at the playground, okay?" He hoped the dragon would say yes.

The dragon nodded solemnly.

Ben took a few steps, then turned back to ask one more question.

"Excuse me, what's your name?"

"I am *Ambroise*."

"My name's Ben—Benjamin."

"Well met, Ben-Benjamin."

"No," the boy said, "just Ben."

The dragon's eyes glowed a friendly blue-green. Ambroise bowed his crystal scaled head.

"It pleases me to see you, Ben."

"Yep." Ben hesitated. "Can I maybe see you tomorrow?"

Ambroise's image wavered with another breeze.

"I am able to visit this place a number of your 'days' before the current close-time ceases to be."

Ben looked back one more time at the seated dragon floating in the gently-moving water.

"Okay," he waved. "Bye!"

The boy ran uphill to the playground.

Ben and the Dragon

Chapter 2 – Do Dragons Exist?

Ben skipped to the kitchen and sat on a stool at the small brown table in the middle of the room. His mother was making dinner.

"What 'cha cookin'?" he asked.

"Chicken Cordon bleu, purée and broccoli," his mother replied.

"Alright! My favorite! Thanks, Mom!"

"*De rien*, Benjamin."

His mother opened the oven to check on roasting chicken, then stirred potatoes, butter and milk together

15

in a bowl on top of the stove. Ben hopped off the stool and went over to the side of the stove where he placed one hand on the stove's edge and one hand on the counter top above the silverware drawer. He pushed himself up, doing body lifts like a gymnast on parallel bars.

"Ben!" his mother said. "The stove is hot. Be careful."

He did a few more lifts, and then hung with his feet swinging. "Mom, do dragons exist?"

The woman tapped a spoon on the edge of the bowl. She wiped her finger on the spoon and licked it. She was accustomed to questions of this sort from her younger son.

"There are stories of dragons in history," she said. "In Great Britain, France, of course, China, Ireland and many other countries. They all have legends that describe these creatures."

Ben frowned. "Yeah—but do they exist?"

"*I've* never seen one," his mother replied, "yet."

"Okay, Mom. Thanks!"

Ben dropped to the floor and ran into the living room where he'd been playing with Charlie, their neighbor, who was visiting before dinner. Charlie would go back home as soon as the Weimers began to eat. He lived two houses away. Charlie's family already ate their supper.

Having played for a while with their Lego City, which dominated the family's dining room, Gui asked his mother for permission to toss the football outside with Ben and Charlie for a few minutes before dinner.

Once in the front yard, Ben took the opportunity to ask his brother whether or not he thought dragons were real.

"No," Gui said, quite sure of himself. "Maybe Komodo Dragons, but *real* dragons don't exist." Gui was twelve, and felt sure about what he knew.

Later that evening, after his shower, Ben trotted down squeaking wooden stairs to his father's office corner in the living room.

"Hi, Dad!"

The boy's father finished typing a sentence he was working on and swiveled his chair to face his younger son.

"All showered up?"

"Yeah…" Ben picked up a plastic letter opener from the side table where his father, a bookseller, packaged books for shipping.

"Dad?"

"Hmm?"

"Do dragons exist?"

"I hope so."

"No, I mean *really*."

His father leaned forward to tap Ben's chest. "My favorite stories are about dragons. But why are you asking me this?"

"Umm…." Ben was a little afraid to say but decided to tell his father. "I don't know—I guess I kind of saw one in the water today."

"You saw a dragon in the water? Now *that's* something."

"What do you mean?"

"It's not the usual tale. I'd be very interested to hear what happens next."

"What's going to happen, Dad?" Ben asked, somewhat worried.

His father smiled. "Probably an adventure. That's my guess. And *this* one starts with you seeing a dragon in the water… hmm."

The boy put the letter opener down. "Yeah," he sighed. "Well Dad, good night." He hugged his father longer than usual.

The man hugged his son, and then patted his back. "'Night, Ben."

Ben ran upstairs to his bedroom. He shared it with Gui now, while his dad was fixing and painting his brother's room. Mom was waiting there, too. They said their nighttime prayers. After the door clicked shut, both boys laid side-by-side in their separate beds, Gui thinking about his favorite football team, the Pittsburgh Steelers, and Ben thinking about Ambroise. He was determined to meet the dragon again the next day after school. He wasn't *quite* sure it had really happened....

Chapter 3 – ANOTHER WORLD

Three more days of school before Christmas break!

And *this* day promised to be cool and sunny. Since waking, Ben thought constantly of Ambroise. While eating cereal and sitting on the couch in the living room, he asked his mother if they could go to the park again after school.

Gui was lying on the floor under a blanket covering a heater vent. He basked in the furnace warmth. "We went yesterday," he complained, eyes shut.

"Pleeease, Mom!" Ben said.

The mother gave a look to her older son and told Ben yes.

"Thank you sooo much!"

Ben jumped off the couch and ran over to give his mother a hug. Mike, their English Labrador, lifted his head from the floor. His eyebrows moved as he looked from mother to son.

After an eternal bus ride home from school, just at four o'clock, when the double doors opened, Ben raced down the tall steps and jumped up to hug his mother at the end of the concrete driveway. Gui followed more slowly. Mike sniffed both boys, wagging his tail as the bus drove off.

"Can we go to the park now?" Ben asked.

His mother gave Gui a welcome-home hug. "After your snack. Dad wants to walk Mike."

"Alright!"

The family van, a Pontiac Montana, rolled to a stop on the side of the gravel trail between the picnic shelter closer to the pond and a hillside playground. Ben slid the side door open, unbuckling his seat belt.

"Can I go to the pond?"

His father was searching for a retractable dog leash between the front seats. "Don't get your feet wet," he said.

"I won't!"

The boy was already running downhill.

He raced to the spot where he'd been standing the previous day. It felt like a year since he'd last seen the shadow. He couldn't believe it was only yesterday.

This Monday afternoon was slightly cloudy, although sunny. It was cool but not cold. A week and a half until Christmas, and no snow had fallen yet.

As his breathing slowed, the boy scanned the water with his sharp young eyes. He spotted a first minnow darting away from his shadow near the water's edge.

No sign of the dragon.

A breeze was blowing ripples on the pond's surface. Holding his breath and looking for some sign of the magic creature, tears welled up in his eyes from not blinking. He didn't want to blink or even breathe because it would feel like giving up.

After counting to one hundred, he closed his stinging eyes. He had blinked a couple of times. His shoulders drooped.

A deep crystal tone rumbled from the pond. "Hello, Benjamin."

"Ambroise!" Ben whispered, moving closer to the pond's edge. "Where *were* you?"

"Your atmospheric currents disturb the surface of this liquid. When that occurs, I am unable to approach until it is once again still."

"Well," Ben said, "I'm glad to see you!"

"And I, you," the dragon replied.

"I wish I could be in *your* world."

With faceted turquoise eyes, Ambroise regarded the boy. "You may, if you are adventurous enough."

Ben squatted and poked at the mud. He watched the water at the edge grow cloudy.

Ambroise lowered his long neck. "As I told you, we may exchange realities."

"You mean you can come *here*, to Flushing?" Ben could just imagine a dragon flying over their house!

"Yes; I will be you."

"Wait! What?" the boy asked.

The shadow dragon straightened regally. "I will *be* you, Benjamin, *in your stead*."

"Oh." Ben didn't want to say 'planet' or 'world' again because it seemed a little scary. "What about when I go to where *you* are?"

"You will inhabit my appearance," Ambroise replied.

Ben had to ask his next question. It's what he'd been hoping ever since he started to understand what the dragon was telling him. "And I would be you? I could *fly* like you?"

"All that I am and can do, you would be and could do," the dragon rumbled.

Oh my gosh, the boy thought. He stared across the pond.

He looked back, afraid that Ambroise would be gone. The sparkling, floating image was still there. He looked to see where his family was.

Dad was walking Mike on the uphill part of the path. Gui was swinging and Mom was getting something from the van.

"How do I come back?" he whispered, facing the water dragon once again.

"The same as during our first translation," the dragon answered. "We must touch the smooth boundary simultaneously. At that moment, our awarenesses will exchange once again."

Ben didn't understand completely, but it was alright. Just the *idea* sounded great, and besides, he trusted Ambroise. With a quick breath, he refocused on the only important thing: *he* could be a dragon—and *fly*!

As a bonus, if he were in Ambroise's world, then he wouldn't have to go to school....

That helped to make the whole idea irresistible.

"What if I get stuck there? What if you get stuck here? I don't want to leave my family."

"Our legends of your world are fascinating. But as you say, I, too, have no wish to leave my own 'family.'

"Three of your days remain," the dragon continued, "before our worlds part." Its crystal image faded as a light breeze brushed the surface of the pond. "I will not willingly risk being stuck in your world, Benjamin."

This felt *exactly* like standing in his inline skates on the edge of the half-pipe at the Wheeling skate park, only more so. Ben's memories replayed how great it was to finally glide smoothly down the ramp and then up, almost floating....

He heard the echo of his father's voice in his head. *You only have to be brave this one time, Ben.*

Boy....

One thing for sure—he couldn't wait to come back and tell his brother and mom and dad and friends all about being in a dragon's world!

And, he could miss the rest of school, and not go to Mrs. Wojtasek's third grade class at Saint Mary's Central Catholic School until after New Year's.

Ben's heart was pounding. "Okay. I can do it," he said.

Ambroise's eyes shifted purple-violet. "Very well. With these atmospheric conditions, I sense we must translate immediately. For safety, please return here tomorrow at this same star position."

"Star position?" Ben asked.

"Your star is above and behind you," Ambroise rumbled. "Return tomorrow at this same... arrangement. When you are in Diamant, peer into the reflective surface of the pool and fix this scene in your mind. You will find that we dragons have... exceptional memories."

Ben's belly was queasy with excitement. "Okay. What do I do now?"

The boy knew his dad was probably done walking Mike. Gui had already yelled down to his younger brother twice.

"Enter the liquid and touch my image without disturbing the surface. We must translate only when our images are stable."

"Dad told me not to get wet!"

"This is required," the dragon said.

Ben hesitated, then nodded. *I'm sorry, Dad.* "Can we do it *now*?"

"Yes," the dragon replied. "Slowly."

Ben stepped into the squishy mud. It was *so* cold. Ambroise's shadow hovered beyond where he could reach. He took another careful step. His feet and ankles felt as though they were immersed in snow.

"Steadily," the baritone voice rumbled from the shadow, much closer.

Ben took another step into the icy water which was up to his knees. He couldn't believe how cold it was! He reached out with one finger. Ambroise's image extended a crystalline neck toward the boy. *Almost there....*

"Benjamin!"

Ben flinched. His dad was *much* closer than expected, and he didn't sound happy.

"Yes!?" the boy's high voice rang out. The freezing water was over his knees, his feet were sinking into the muck, his heart was pounding and he saw Ambroise's crystal eyes, deep green and very close, just in front of his trembling hand. He touched a fingertip slowly to the water, right on the dragon's nose.

"*Get ooout ooove tthhhe waaaterrr....*" His father's voice faded, faded... faded.

Then blackness.

Ben and the Dragon

Chapter 4 – CHANGED

Ambroise landed on his rump, his tailless rump. He took a deep, surprised breath and... *cold?*

Yes. That was the word. *Wet*, too. A rushing flood of experience and information filled his mind. He stood on two (!) unfamiliar legs. He backed, slipping, awkwardly through the mud and onto shore.

Everything was cold and wet and overpowering. His form was utterly unusual—no stabilizing tail, no wings. His neck was so short that it felt as if his head was attached directly to his torso.

He felt *so* bare. If it hadn't been for the familiar feeling of the boy's mind, Ambroise was certain he would have retreated within himself in shock.

The dragon trembled—it was this body's reaction to immersion in the frigid liquid of the "pond." Knowing how cold it had been for the man-child, Ambroise was amazed that Ben had actually done his part for their translation.

"*What* are you doing, Ben?" the boy's father shouted, running down to the shivering, wet figure.

Ambroise's small head shook itself left and right. Hesitation and unfamiliarity with human vocalization spanned many heartbeats...

§

"Ooooohh," Ben thought.

He couldn't breathe!

Help! He couldn't speak! His mouth didn't work! Everything was dark and fluorescent, neon and glow-in-the-dark.

The boy stepped back—with four feet!—feeling a long tail lift itself gracefully while two huge wings spread wide for balance. His strange new body—a very large one—automatically balanced itself. What power!

A big blue glowing moon—*Vagabonder*—hung directly overhead and a small, black pool at his feet—actually he had powerful, scaled legs ending in diamond-tipped claws—showed a familiar, hazy scene.

That must be his pond in Flushing! And a boy—*me,* Ben thought—was sitting in the mud at the edge of the water. *Get up!* Ben voicelessly strained. *Come on!*

He saw his father hurry down the hillside to the boy figure. There were far-away sounds of voices. The man helped the boy stand. Ben could see himself shivering. *Oh, boy. I hope he's okay.*

"Dad!" Ben tried to shout. "I'm here!"

Instead of his own voice, a strange rumbling emanated from… from his chest? No words emerged from his mouth. He opened and closed his long jaw of shining, sharp crystal teeth; he licked them with his forked tongue.

Of course, dragons didn't speak like humans. He *knew* that now. No sounds come from their mouths; *that's* where they breathe fire from.

As with Ambroise in Ben's world, the boy's reaction to his surroundings was eased by a flood of reassuring memories. If it hadn't been for the flow of dragon *knowing*, Ben's mind would have spun away, or curled up, panicking from the rush of strange sensations.

The boy dragon peered into the pool as first his father, then Guillaume, then his mother, and then Mike entered the field of view around his boy self.

Ben's father picked up the boy—it was so strange to watch himself from the outside—and his family hurried uphill to their waiting van. Ben remained for several minutes, watching the empty pond scene from the edge of the black pool. The images blurred and then refocused. Not with tears; his crystalline faceted eyes were incapable of producing liquid. It was the wind blowing over the surface of the pond back in Flushing.

A deep, natural calm, native to Diamant's dragons, reassured the eight-year-old boy. He reluctantly moved away to examine this strange new familiar world....

Chapter 5 – Vegetables and Blow-ups

Ambroise was immersed in a whirlwind of voices, emotions, movement and activity. If it weren't for the *familiarity* of these things, he would have retreated from the chaos. He felt deeply reassured, however. This boy's body knew it was safe.

After the short ride home in the family van shivering under his father's coat, Ambroise was carried inside their dwelling, examined, taken upstairs, undressed and placed in a "hot shower." The water he found himself in *this* time was warm. Oh, yes. The trembling of his body subsided as he stood under the shower of warmth. He breathed in the steam.

On the other side of a waterproof shower curtain, mother, brother and father sat and stood around in the bathroom, asking questions. Their family dog lay in the hallway outside the door. Ambroise heard himself speak for the first time with a human voice.

"I'm okay," he answered.

"I don't know," he said.

"I'm sorry, Mom," he heard himself say.

"I didn't mean to make you worry."

"Yes. I saw something in the water."

These things were said nearly automatically by the dragon's new body and mind.

"What did you see in the water?" the father pursued.

"A dragon," Ambroise replied through the soothing steam.

"What are you talking about, Ben?"

"I saw a dragon," Ambroise said.

"What do you mean?" Gui asked, trying to help his parents. He was sitting on the wobbly chair next to the linen pantry. "Why do you keep saying drag-oon?"

"I saw a *dragon* in the water," Ambroise's new, high-pitched voice stated, somewhat tiredly.

"Was it a fish?" the father asked.

"No—it was a dragon."

Ben's father nodded when the boy's mother silently prompted him to stop his questioning. "Well, you just clean up and get warm."

Once he was dry and dressed in clean clothes, the dragon was able to focus. This human body, an immature male, possessed a complete life and position in this family unit.

Two other species shared their home. A white "dog" and two feline sisters. Three species combined to make one family unit. *Fascinating*, the dragon thought.

In the living room, Gui knelt in front of an open textbook on the floor. Ambroise sat on the couch. The dragon held his arms straight out, after moving each of them in every possible range. He blinked several times with his new eyes and felt the soft skin on the sides of his face with his fingers. He felt his hair. He stood, wobbling.

His older brother finally noticed the dragon's self-examination. Gui frowned and then looked back down to write out vocabulary definitions with a pencil.

"Ben?" his mother called from the kitchen.

"Yes?" Ambroise answered, amazed again at the high timbre of his new voice.

"Do you have to read your story tonight?"

"Yes," he heard himself say.

The dragon walked to his backpack and removed a book. He carried it into the room where his mother was preparing their evening meal. He sensed that she was worried.

"It's okay, Mom," he said.

The mother stirred a steaming pot on the stove. *Everything* seemed to involve water in this place! Ambroise had squeezed the soft skin of his legs and arms in the shower. He was simply *made* from water.

His mother studied her son's face. "Well," she motioned to the book in his hands, "go on."

Ambroise found himself "reading" aloud from a book whose subject was… dragons.

"*Coincidence? I think not!*" A line of dialogue from a movie the family enjoyed sounded ironically in his head.

Dragons did not record facts artificially—either on paper, carved on something, or with a "computer." They had perfect, complete recall. Ambroise was surprised to realize something he already knew from

Ben's mind: humans depend almost entirely on artificial recordings to maintain their cultural narrative over the centuries.

They also lived very short lives—only as old as he was now—and remembered nearly nothing. *A shame*, he thought.

The Dragon's Apprentice was a young reader's book in a series called *The Dragonology Chronicles*. It was imaginative—this fact alone was remarkable. Although most of its focus was on the humans, the story involved their two species enmeshed in a web of action and intrigue that he assumed eight-year-old human children were expected to find interesting.

His liquid eyes followed the lines of characters, and a surprisingly clear, small voice read aloud the story of creatures reminiscent of his own kind. *Fascinating....*

So simple.

Yet nearly beyond description! Were he to attempt to convey what he was going through to his brethren, the dragon wasn't sure he would succeed. There existed no common ground of experience; his kind was made of entirely different matter. And his own species invented nothing "make believe" or fictional, as he definitely knew this story to be.

Ambroise found everything fuller and richer than his imaginings had been; he was experiencing, from within, another creature's life, and not simply observing it from the outside.

The dragon book was wrong in every detail, of course. As a third-grader, he was required to read it aloud to his family for school. It wouldn't be wise, he thought, to reveal how much he knew of this book's inaccuracies....

At a chapter's end, the dragon said, "That's all I have to read tonight, Mom."

"Okay, sweetie."

Ambroise got up from the stool at the center table and approached the stove. "What are you cooking?"

"Green beans with tomatoes for me; broccoli and a cauliflower casserole in the oven for you, your dad and your brother. No meat tonight. Well, there *are* bacon bits in the casserole."

"Okay," the dragon said.

Ben's mother looked at her son. She ran her fingers through his hair and felt his forehead.

"Mom, I'm fine," the dragon said.

She hugged Ambroise. "Don't worry, Ben. I won't make you eat my tomatoes and green beans."

Ambroise had been focusing on just those cooking odors, and his face frowned at her reassuring words. "Uumm. Actually Mom, I was hoping—could I please have some?"

His mother's eyebrows rose. "Green beans?"

The dragon nodded his small head, looking up. "Yes, please… and tomatoes."

"Okay, sweetie. If that's what you want."

§

With his dragon's steady gaze, Ambroise took it all in—eating, breathing, everything—and forgot nothing. He was amazed at dinner by the sensations and tastes of actual physical eating. Imagine! Placing physical material in his body! *This* is what the legends had described.

Knowing everything that Ben knew, the dragon was aware that he didn't like certain foods, especially the non-meat items—in particular, tomatoes. But Ambroise couldn't resist. He ate as many of the vegetables as he could, even asking Gui to surrender his untouched cauliflower.

Both brother and parents were surprised at Ambroise's behavior. This wasn't the Ben *they* knew....

§

Immediately following dinner, almost to the minute, the front doorbell rang. Gui looked up from his iPad and peered through the sidelight of the front door. "Charlie's here! Get the door, Ben."

The dragon jogged over to unlock the deadbolt. He swung the door open past a row of shoes with jackets hung above them.

"Hey, Charlie," Ambroise said.

"Hey, Ben." Charlie took off his coat.

"Guys," Gui said, throwing down his iPad and jumping up from the couch, "let's go out and pass the ball!" He jammed his feet into his shoes and shrugged his coat on.

"Yeah!" Charlie exclaimed, pulling his own coat back on.

Gui turned to Ambroise, "Ben, ask Mom if we can toss the ball in front." He pushed through the storm door.

The dragon walked with his strange new feet through the kitchen and into his mother's art studio, a former attached garage. He stood in the doorway. His mother was painting a holiday scene for an art class she would be teaching later in the week. After a final stroke of black on the snowman's top hat, she looked up with brush and palette in hand.

"Yes, Ben?"

"Charlie's here," Ambroise said. "Can Guillaume, Charlie and I toss the ball in the front yard?"

His mother gave her son a relieved smile. "Okay. Be careful and keep away from the road."

"We will."

After putting his own coat on, Ambroise went out front to where Gui and Charlie were waiting. His older brother was tossing the football to himself in dramatic fashion.

"What did Mom say?"

The dragon shrugged. "She said to be careful and keep away from the road."

Gui threw the ball up extra high. "Come on guys! Let's play Interception.…"

Ambroise followed the other boys into the approaching dusk. The darkness was reminiscent of his dragon home world.

"Hey, Ben! Plug in the blow-ups!" Gui jumped to catch the ball in 'touchdown' style in the middle of the yard.

"Yeah, blow-ups!" echoed Charlie, hopping excitedly.

The dragon saw four separate extension cords on the front porch. He kneeled in front of the first outlet.

"Blow-ups! Blow-ups!" Charlie chanted.

Ambroise plugged in two cords. A humming sound and glowing, many-colored lights sprung into being. He stood, transfixed. Though a pale imitation, these colors reminded him of his own world. "Blow-up" fan motors were reminiscent of his *Gardien's* soothing rumble....

His eyes stung. The dragon was surprised to feel 'homesick.' This body certainly experienced powerful emotions.

"Come on, Ben! Plug in the snowman. Let's go!" Gui's shouting brought Ambroise out of his reverie. "Charlie, cover me. Ready? Set—hike."

Ambroise plugged in the remaining two cords on the other side of the porch. More fan sounds and colored lights.

For the next twenty minutes in the growing darkness, the hundred-year-old former crystal dragon chased and ran along with the other boys, throwing and catching a football and shouting, "Here!"

He relaxed into the present, giggling and tackling his brother and Charlie. Playing was *fun*.

The night air felt refreshing in his nose and lungs. His hands and face were warm from physical activity.

The three boys played in the darkness on the grass between the inflatable Santa, a snowman and three spinning penguins. Their breath steamed in the night air. Ambroise enjoyed laughing as much as playing "Interception."

Fascinating, a distant part of his mind commented.

Ben and the Dragon

Chapter 6 – Flying & Flames

Crystal diamonds?

Examining his new body, Ben saw his overlapping scales were made of diamonds or different colored iridescent crystals. They were nearly indestructible, he knew. He turned from the small black pool. Its liquid—not water, but *L'essence,* his dragon memory supplied the name—rose from deep beneath the surface of Diamant.

Two things were obvious. It was night, and every single question he would have wanted to ask was already answered by his dragon mind. It felt like riding on Dad's shoulders, but on the *inside,* and he didn't feel like he was going to fall off. Everything he wanted to know, he already knew as soon as he wondered about it.

And really, "night" wasn't right. This side of the dragon's world was in perpetual twilight because of its slow rotation and the reflected sunlight from six orbiting moons. The planet's blue star, *Vega,* as humans called it, accounted for the unique moonlight hue.

It was like being inside of a know-it-all machine, Ben thought. He flexed his barbed tail.

His hind legs and forelegs were powerfully muscled. His long neck allowed him to turn his head all the way around to examine every part of his body. Ben spent some time doing just that, looking over his own spiny back.

He furled and unfurled large wings. Held up, they were shimmering sheets of miniature diamonds. How big were they? How big was *he*? Surprisingly, this was not something he could *know*. There was nothing here to compare to—no cars, no houses and no boy's hands to hold wide and show to parents.

He was bigger. It seemed like he was looking down from higher than Dad's ten-foot stepladder. From his dragon's memory he knew how large he was compared to *Gardien*, but... What? Ambroise's mom and dad were all in one creature? Yes. He *knew* this was true.

A *Gardien* was a single overseer and protector to each youngling... Youngling?

Yes.

Ambroise was a hundred years old, but to immortal dragons, that was a drop in the ocean of time, which wasn't at all the same thing for dragons. Youngling....

Wow. Ambroise is a kid, like me, Ben thought. Now the boy knew that his dragon friend was calm and mature-seeming because crystal dragons always were like that.

He also knew that each *Gardien* (all mature dragons become *Gardiens*) was one thousand years old and older. It didn't matter how much older than a thousand years because dragons lived forever in this world. On Diamant, there were younglings and *Gardiens*. Before a thousand years, you were a kid.

He could spend forever thinking about everything he knew now. Ben's—Ambroise's—*Gardien* was twice as tall as he was....

The boy felt fear at that thought, but was reassured by his dragon mind; he was protected and safe. And now, he could fly!

It was much darker than back home, but Ben felt none of his usual anxiety at the lack of light. Three moons, *Lune*, *Ryvasser* and *Vagabonder*, were visible. The first two were just above the rocky horizon. *Vagabonder* was directly overhead, a 'high moon,' and it felt very... inviting.

Ben stretched experimentally. Yes... he could.... he would... *eat* moonlight? He realized he knew that crystal dragons of Diamant absorbed moonlight through their wings. Hey! They were solar powered! Moon-powered? Dad would love that.

The boy *needed* to fly. An inner urge was growing more insistent. Thinking of moons had brought up the memory of how satisfying *repas* was. Dragons eat while flying. At home, Dad always told him, *never chew food and run around*, ever since he choked on a hotdog while jumping....

Poised on the barren rock surface of Diamant, wings flexed in anticipation, Ben *felt* every one of the hundred years of his life in this world. *Now!* it called to him.

Crouching, claws gripping rock, wing flexors tensed. With a mighty spring, his dragon body launched straight up into the sky—what must be 50 feet on Earth!

Iridescent wings beat powerfully at the twilight world's atmosphere. The ground shrunk below. This was like being on the biggest, fastest elevator in the universe!

The air wasn't cold. It wasn't anything. It blew past his streamlined head and his eyes were not affected at all by his incredible speed because they were crystal. Ben surrendered to his urge to climb higher. He stretched his neck.

This was how dragons felt hungry! It was different from how his stomach felt as a boy when he was hungry and he smelled something good cooking. This was not his stomach.... What? He didn't even have one?!

His stomach-less hunger was an all-over feeling, like an itch *before* it itched.

Stone hills, valleys and rolling plains were so far below that he remembered the first time he flew in a jet. His wings stretched wide, causing his crystalline body to seemingly coast level.

Uummmmm.

In the mornings, under a blanket covering the heater vent in the living room in the winter—*that's* how this felt. Sooooo good. Ben felt better and better and better.

After a long time—like after a reaaally long drink at the drinking fountain when they came in from recess playing tag at school—he felt *full.* He was done. And he *was* full, but he hadn't eaten a thing!

Graceful wings beat again against the moonlit air to regain lost altitude. Ben searched the horizon. He *knew* he was *sud* from home—Ambroise's home—and flying in *that* direction would take him twenty minutes to get there. This new time sense was awesome. Like smelling something or seeing a familiar color, he *knew* where he was in time. There was no guessing. He was a flying clock!

Just then, Ben hit a wall of soundless noise lasting several wing beats. *Come*, it rumbled through his wings and chest.

Gardien!

Breathing deeply through slits in his thorax, Ben heard his own dragon voice blast out a long reply. His wings beat on steadily and he veered toward the distant line of peaks.

I'm going to meet Ambroise's mom, he thought, slightly worried.

Each second was flying further from *his* home. The total reassurance from his dragon self helped so much. *Everything is fine*, it told him. He sure hoped so.

§

Flames!

Brilliant blue flames shot from several openings in the rock mountain.

As he spiraled down to the familiar unfamiliar mountain side, Ben knew what it was. *Gardien* was cleaning their lair with fire, vaporizing crystal dust.

Oh man! Mom would love that. Their dog, Mike, shed hair all the time, and it would be great if Mom could use a fire to clean the same as Ambroise's *Gardien*.

The boy reminisced about using the vacuum at home to suck up dust, hair and... other things like Lego pieces from stairways and corners. Maybe *Gardien* would let him—

Wait! Yes he could! He *could* breathe fire!

Diamond wings blasted the air powerfully downward once, twice, and with a final push, hind claws touched down on the rock outside the main cave entrance. Wings folded as he dropped to all fours. Ben moved forward eagerly, yet somewhat fearfully, into the darkened lair tunnel.

Ben and the Dragon

Chapter 7 – WORLDS APART

Both boy and dragon had adventurous first nights in their new world.

Ambroise was experiencing what it felt like to be made of waterborne flesh. Eliminating water and other matter in the strangely-named "bathroom" was unexpected, to say the least.

Experiencing his first nightly prayer with his mother and brother before "going to sleep" also piqued the dragon's curiosity. His boy's mind was reassured by this nighttime ritual.

Together they offered thanks for the day; asked for sick friends and family to be healthy; asked for success in their parents' lives and for all people to go to heaven. They asked that the boys have good dreams and wake in the morning "fresh as daisies" as his mother always put it. All of this addressed to "God," which felt like *Gardien* to Ambroise.

In the darkened room, under a blanket, wearing 'PJ's' and resting his new round head on a pillow, the dragon was finding everything new.

"Night," his brother said.

Gui was on his own bed to the dragon's right, his blanket smoothed perfectly and his hands folded on his chest.

"Goodnight, Gui," Ambroise said.

After ten minutes, the dragon heard his brother's breathing become deep and regular. A slight snoring sound accompanied each in-breath.

Ambroise found himself doing something he'd never done as a dragon. His mouth opened wide, eyes closed, chest rose as he inhaled deeply, then slowly, he breathed out, eyes watering. It felt *very* satisfying. He understood from Ben's mind that this was a sign he was "tired."

He yawned again.

In the boy's memory, Ambroise found a surprising fact that he already knew: he "slept" every night for nine or ten hours! *How peculiar.*

The dragon then began drifting *away…* to another place. It was disconcerting. To the boy's mind, this transition was accepted and completely normal, although not understood or thought of. It *was*. People slept.

And *this* is where the dragon's night of adventures began. He was in for quite a surprise because he had never been asleep before, let alone dream….

§

Ben's own adventures continued as he walked slowly through the entrance tunnel into the main chamber of the dragon's lair.

Ambroise's *Gardien* was huge! *Oh my gosh*, Ben thought, looking up at the massive dragon who regarded him with large turquoise crystal eyes. Enormous wings lay folded on its back. Blue sparks floated through the air, embers sifting down before winking out.

"So," *Gardien* rumbled, chest vents opening with sound, "what are *you* called in your world?"

Ben was afraid of Ambroise's protector. He also felt calmly reassured; his dragon mind told him he was safe. He knew he could share any information with *Gardien*.

Dragons were fearlessly honest and never, ever lied. All of them were fearless, not just *Gardiens*. What *could* a dragon be afraid of, anyway?

Okay. The boy addressed Ambroise's *Gardien*. "I'm Ben, Benjamin Weimer," he said.

Ben knew his own heartbeat would have been crazy-fast. Inside his dragon self, all he felt was a curious fluttering in his chest whenever he "spoke" through his vents; they reminded him of the gills on a shark.

"You are a stranger to Diamant," *Gardien* said, "but Ambroise's memories and mind pattern will serve you well. You have discovered this already." The massive dragon leaned over to peer at the boy. "Why did you agree to come here? You are quite young for your kind, I suspect."

Ben felt his eight-year-old self adopting a direct and dragon-like way of thinking. His body walked into the large chamber and curled itself near a glowing blue wall. His tail encircled folded limbs. He gestured with a scaled chin as he spoke in the dragon's language without noticing.

"I first saw Ambroise's shadow in the pond and couldn't believe that dragons actually existed. And I wanted to see what it's like here. I wanted to fly, and maybe breathe fire. And…" Ben arrived at his main reason for coming to the dragon world.

He looked down at the stone floor and lowered his scaled head. "….I didn't want to go to school again before Christmas. When Ambroise told me we could change places, I knew I wouldn't have to go to school because *he* would be me and I could be here and, you know, have fun."

"Hhmmmmm," *Gardien* rumbled, eyes pale blue. The dragon rose to its full height. "What is your current stage of development?"

Ben's dragon memory let him know that *Gardien* was asking how old he was.

"I'm eight. I'll be nine in…" The boy looked down at his claws. He knew how many days there were until

Christmas and until the end of the month, and then seventeen days in January…. "Thirty-one days!" he rumbled proudly. "I'll be nine in thirty-one days."

"Nine… *years*," *Gardien* replied. "I thought so. This is the approximate age, in your comparative scale, of our Ambroise."

The adult dragon reached down to touch Ben's head with its own slender jaw. "I suspect your time in our world will be instructive and even 'fun.' You are welcome in this *crèche*. Everything you desire to know may be found in Ambroise's memory. I sense that you have recently experienced *festoyé* by *Vagabonder* moonlight."

"Yes," Ben nodded. He would have asked, *Why do dragons eat light?* But he already knew. It would be awesome back home! Everything he wanted to know, all of his questions, were instantly known. Dragons were so lucky! And they remembered *everything* without even trying.

Maybe that's another reason why I was able to come here, he thought. Mom has a great memory; it's pretty dragon-like. And in school, he remembered things easily, too.

Ben realized he was starting to think about himself like a dragon would think about an alien—which he was! He also *knew* this would happen more and more, the longer he remained here.

What if I do get stuck here? would have been his next question. Would it be so bad?

The calm of *Gardien's* voice… and everything… felt right. There were no worries. This dragon pattern was very strong and… *no! I want to see Mom and Dad and Gui and Charlie and Mike and the cats!*

"You are no doubt aware," *Gardien* rumbled, addressing the boy's thoughts, "That if you fail to make your return translation, both of you will be *échoué*—stranded—in each other's lives.

"A pattern of being is powerful, like a heavy world, and you *will* be pulled into it, the longer you stay. It will be difficult for you to maintain your own mental organization. It will be no less difficult for Ambroise in your world.

"Come," *Gardien* said kindly, "I will take you to meet someone."

Ben said in a dragon's whisper, "*Ricard.*"

With a nod, *Gardien* moved gracefully, leading him back outside. *Gardien* wasn't a girl, he knew, but it felt nicer to think of her as a 'she.' Ben's long tail waved with each hind leg step.

She led him onto the platform that reminded Ben of the deck behind his house or the aircraft carrier deck in his iPad game, *F18 Carrier Landing.*

He felt more like a dragon each moment. And now he would meet a person who'd come here as he had—and stayed.

One thousand five hundred years ago, in the country known currently as France, Ricard had translated to Diamant.

Ben also knew Ricard could help him stay "himself" until he and Ambroise translated back. A long waking night stood between now and then. Dragons don't sleep, so there was plenty of time for…. What did humans call it? Ah, yes… *fun.*

§

Dragons never age physically after one-thousand-years—that is when they become Gardiens.

Ben and the Dragon

Chapter 8 – A New Day

The next morning, Ambroise lie awake. He blinked occasionally. It was 5:30.

Before last night, he had assumed that these humans' "sleep" cycles were simply stretches of empty time. Dragons don't sleep, and the notion that someone would be inactive for such a long period each day had been incomprehensible. But last night....

The family will awaken at six when the parents' alarm goes off. His dragon senses had carried over and he was able to detect time intervals even though his mind was preoccupied with last night's "dreaming."

Dragons never sleep—their revitalization comes during *festoyé*. Because Ambroise was essentially a dragon, even though he was in a boy's body, he had not "slept" during last night's dreaming!

Inactivity? No. That is the wrong word for what humans experience while sleeping. During one single night, Ambroise had lived through days upon adventurous days in the boy's dreaming mind.

Playing in the snow with his brother, his parents and Mike; sledding down hills in the sky; going to school and playing with his friends on a pirate ship; acrobatic skating in the Wheeling skate park and the Wheeling Heritage Port on the Ohio River; frightening encounters with dozens of imaginary and real creatures of varying description, including dinosaurs; hugging ultra-soft stuffed animals; riding amusement park rides through the Saint Clairsville Wal-Mart, and on and on.

Ambroise shook his small head. Humans lived in *two* worlds.

His older brother lie sleeping in the bed beside the dragon. He had spoken once during the night, "waking" Ambroise from the dreaming of his host's mind. The dragon had replied, but the older boy resumed his steady breathing without saying another word. *Curious.* Ambroise wondered what Gui had been experiencing in his own sleeping world.

It was an aspect of human reality that was totally unexpected and... wonderful. Ambroise sat up and hung his feet over the edge of the bed. He regarded his soft, five-toed feet, flexing them and rotating them at the ankles, wiggling his toes.

Feeling a now-familiar urge, Ambroise got up and padded to the bathroom. Afterward, he stood at the sink and enthusiastically brushed his small, flattened teeth. As Benjamin's mind understood it, this activity was for hygiene. "Cavities" were a feared consequence of improper maintenance—to be more accurate, it was the repair work performed by dentists which held the fear.

Crystal dragons never had "cavities." They didn't brush their teeth or their hair—they had no hair. They never became ill. How *fortunate* his kind was.

He savored the taste of toothpaste. In his own world, he didn't "eat" or taste anything. Ever. Consequently, everything he tasted here was interesting.

In front of the vanity, Ambroise picked up his father's hairbrush and smoothed blond hair to one side. He stared into the unchanging color of his liquid eyes. *Fascinating.*

His mother found him standing there as she entered the bathroom. She jumped.

"Ben! You scared me!"

The dragon blinked. "I'm sorry, Mom."

The woman felt her son's forehead. "What are you doing?"

"I used the bathroom and brushed my teeth and hair."

"Is your brother awake?"

"He was sleeping when I got up."

Later, downstairs, holding a bowl of *Life* cereal, the dragon asked his father, who was packaging books for shipping that day, if they could go back to the park after school. The man scrutinized his younger son. "How are you feeling?"

"Good," the dragon said in his boy's voice.

§

During his first waking day in the human world, the activities he took part in were ordinary and reassuring, compared to the previous night's dreaming. With an unblinking gaze the dragon recorded everything.

A pre-dawn school bus ride, walking past darkened seats filled with other morning-quiet children; changing to another bus before arriving at Saint Mary's Central Catholic School at 7:50—this was a pleasant routine. The dreaming world had been chaotic, unpredictable, and at times, frightening.

Peering from his bus window at the buildings and lighted vehicles streaming by in the morning darkness, Ambroise wondered how things were going for Ben in the crystal world of Diamant.

This human environment was feeling more and more familiar. He *felt* so much here. Ambroise felt his resolve to rendezvous with the boy at their respective ponds after school in order to return again to their own worlds fade. The dragon felt as though he were still in a dream.

Chapter 9 – OLD SOULS

"I am like you, young Benjamin," the crimson dragon rumbled, looking down from his greater height.

Ben was impressed. Here was a *human*, in the form of an ancient dragon. He has been here for twenty lifetimes! Ben already knew what he *would* have asked Ricard, but then something occurred to him.

"Do you miss your human home… like I do?"

Seconds stretched into minutes.

"No," the dragon said, returning from long dormant memories. "I, too, was young, as you are, when I translated to Diamant, but I was unhappy. In *Normanz*, my life was passable at times, but I was lonely, and *mes cousines* were not kind to me."

The former boy *Gardien* told Ben of the murder of his parents by Saxon pirates when he was four, and how he was taken in by an uncle whose older children were cruel.

"Six years after my parents' deaths, I was staring into a deep tidal pool on the beach far from my new home one afternoon. I knew not where I would find myself, but I was leaving my uncle's family.

"And then, I saw an unusual shadow. I spoke to that image and told it of my wish to be elsewhere, anywhere else.

"The shadow was my lonely imagination—I thought. I was not a happy boy. My parents were gone and I had no feelings of home anymore. I thought the dragon I saw was not real."

Ricard paused. "The young dragon who translated into my life *en Normanz* never returned before the closing day of *Temps-rapproché.*"

"I waited by the *l'eau* pool until the close-time ended. Not wanting to return to my uncle, I still didn't want to strand someone else in that place. In the end, of course, I remained in Diamant. Now, I *am* home."

Ricard's eyes darkened to sunset red. "My dragon was an adventurous youngling—all younglings who take the step into another realm are—like your Ambroise.

"I was told by my dragon's *Gardien*, and know from my borrowed memories, that he held no desire to abandon his life."

Ricard the dragon whispered, "I will never know what happened to him."

If Ben had been in his own body, he would have hugged this huge dragon. Instead, he lightly tapped his crystal-scaled head on the ancient *Gardien's* huge wing —it was the dragon way of showing understanding and sympathy. "I like Diamant," the boy said, "but I would miss my family a lot."

The crimson dragon nodded. "I, too, missed my parents; I do not wish for you to remain, or for Ambroise to be *échoué* in your life, therefore I will help you."

Ben understood so much from Ambroise's memories. He couldn't sleep in his new dragon form. It was impossible. It was strange not being tired, even though he felt like he should be. He wished he could tell his mom and dad and brother where he was—and hug Mike again. At times it felt overwhelming.

Dragons didn't have to go to bed or eat vegetables, they breathed crystal blue fire, they could fly and they lived forever! And now he could do *all* of these things.

It wasn't fair.

Just when he got everything he ever wanted, he missed his family—he almost couldn't see them in his mind anymore. It was growing harder to remember home.

A deep reassurance flowed into his thoughts from the well of Ambroise's mind. Dragons were so calm! It felt better than hugging the softest teddy bear Ben had in his room....

Gardien's rumbling interrupted the boy's thoughts.

"You must think of your human connections and your family."

"I was!" Ben answered in his dragon voice. "I *am*. It's not easy, though."

Ricard stomped his hind leg. "Yes! We are rooted in ourselves—and because you are only a shadow of yourself in this world—you *will* fade, as you know, the longer you are here. Your old life and self will disappear like a barely-remembered *rêve*."

Lose his mom and dad and brother like a dream? "No!" Ben roared.

Ricard stretched his wings. "It is most important for you to think of your family and remember your feelings for them even if it is difficult. You must stay 'awake' to them. And you must have as much 'fun' as possible—*Now!*"

The crimson dragon leapt into the moonlit sky.

When Ambroise's *Gardien* had greeted Ricard earlier, a silent communication had occurred; Ben would stay with Ricard until the next *Vagabonder* high moon. With a lingering touch on the boy's head, his dragon had departed.

For the next ten hours, Ben had *lots* of fun. More fun than he ever thought was possible. The former French boy led Ben higher than any aircraft could fly on Earth. They dove at jet fighter speeds, swooped back up, spinning and turning and stalling. Ricard led Ben through loops, banks and all the aerial moves a crystal dragon could do. The boy already knew of them from Ambroise's mind but he had never *done* them before. Effortless coasting in various shifting layers of moving air. Soaring miles high with no parachute. "Tasting" light from different moons.

They soaked up the moonlight from three minor moons once in *repas*. *This is like recharging batteries*, Ben thought. *But quicker.*

They swooped over stone outcroppings and breathed fire, melting crystal rock into glowing blue liquid glass. *This is* so *fun!* Much better than the best playground time.

He couldn't wait to tell Mom and Dad and Gui and Charlie…. The more fun he had, the more he missed his family and wanted to tell them all about it. *This was why Ricard said he should have fun.* He *knew* that.

Finally, they flew toward the black pool. They banked, circled, swooped down, flared their wings and landed.

Vagabonder was high overhead and it was almost time to re-translate back home. Even one more day…. Ben wasn't too sure he could do it. He really hoped Ambroise would be at the Flushing pond. His boy self was nervous.

"Don't worry, youngling," Ricard rumbled from a rock. The crimson dragon glowed deep red.

"You are an old soul, and this is why you were able to come to our world. Your essence, wiser than its years, resonates with the essence of Diamant. Yet your place is with your *famille*. My memory of your enthusiasm and your youthful joy are gifts I will treasure. My time with you has been a pleasure, Benjamin."

Ricard settled down.

"I'm glad I got to fly with you, too," Ben said. He knew his eyes would have been stinging with tears if he were in his own body—tears of leaving and tears of missing his family and his life as a boy. His faceted crystal eyes remained unblinking. The dragon calm muted most of his emotions.

Ricard curled his long tail and settled his wings into place. "Now I suggest you attend the *l'eau* pool."

The boy spun around.

Nothing but blackness. He stared intently into the reflective pool, willing a connection between their worlds like he willed Christmas morning or the end of a school day to come more quickly into being.

Swirling fog appeared. A pond quietly came into focus. *His* pond. It was snowing!

"It's snowing!" his dragon voice rumbled.

Ricard nodded.

Ben sat expectantly on a rock at the edge of the dark pool.

Chapter 10 – ALMOST HOME

They paused on a steep incline at the intersection of the road his family lived on. The driver turned left and slowed, stopping at the Weimer family house.

Being a boy was not easy.

Ambroise knew he would go inside, eat a snack and have something to drink. He was tired. This body fatigued easily—and recharged almost as rapidly as a dragon in *repas*.

The dragon, carrying his own heavy book bag, followed Gui off the bus. "Bye," he said when he passed the driver.

He went carefully down the high steps—two legs were definitely less stable than his normal four. Once on the driveway, he was hugged by his mother. The bus engine rumble faded.

"How was school?" his mother asked. Mike sniffed the dragon's hands. Ambroise stroked the dog's thick wavy fur.

"Okay," he replied.

"It was good," Gui said. "Mom, guess what? We get to play drums in the Christmas program…"

Ambroise followed his brother, mother and dog down the sidewalk, onto the front porch and through the front door. It was *warm* inside. Dropping his book bag near a row of shoes, Ambroise removed his coat and waited for a break in Gui's talking.

Each moment, it felt more difficult to hold onto his own identity in this boy's body. It was *so* tempting to relax into this life. Diamant seemed far, far away. Like a dream....

"Mom, can we have a snack?" he asked. Needing sleep and physical food, and experiencing a full day of new things at school… it was a lot.

Something whispered it would soon be time for... for what? He couldn't remember.

It had *seemed* important.

§

The concerned mother watched her younger son standing with a far away expression on his face. He was quieter than normal. She resisted feeling his forehead again. Instead, she asked, "Does anyone want hot chocolate?" Ben's face smiled as he nodded. She was relieved at this sign of animation. Although his eyes still seemed distant....

Chapter 11 – Snow

How much better he felt after hot chocolate and a snack! Ambroise relished the flavors of mustard, ketchup, warm bread and 'hot dog.' In the boy's memory there was no information on what hot dogs were, but they were *good*.

The hot chocolate in the bottom of his mug was still warm, and he gratefully sipped, marveling at the richness of tastes. When the dragon set his mug on the kitchen island table, a slight motion outside the back door window caught his eye—snow!

Ambroise jumped up. "It's snowing!"

Gui walked into the kitchen and stood with his nose on the glass of the deck door, intentionally fogging the window. "Waaooow…"

Something in his older brother's joking tone triggered a memory and the dragon shook his head in stunned disbelief. *That's* what he couldn't remember—his own home! Oh, no….

He *must* go back to the pond today.

"Umm—Mom?"

His mother was looking out the kitchen window over the sink. She turned from the view of falling snowflakes. "Yes, sweetie?"

"Can we go to the park?"

"I don't know, Honey."

"Pleeeaase?" Ambroise knew this tone often helped produce results when his parents were reluctant to agree with something.

His mother paused. "Why don't you ask your father?"

"Okay, Mom."

Ambroise opened the basement door and trotted downstairs. "Dad?"

Behind their old deep freezer, standing on a small step ladder, his father dipped a paintbrush into an old plastic juice container. He was painting the window casement white. "How was school, bub?"

"Good—can we go to the park, Dad?"

His father traced the top edge of a board. "Why do you want to go?"

Ambroise gave the only reason he found in the boy's mind. "It's snowing."

"Ah…. Yes. I saw." His father finished the right side of the window and started on the horizontal sill. "There's not enough snow to sled, you know."

Ambroise's attention was drawn to his father's movements—careful strokes on the front of the window frame, brush dipping into paint.... The dragon was mesmerized. What was it he.... *Oh!*

He blinked with urgency and took a deep breath. He was falling asleep—asleep to his own identity. He *must* go! He was losing himself in this boy's life.

"*Dad,*" he said tiredly, almost without hope, "*I need to go.*"

His father stepped down from the ladder. He wiped his brush on a damp rag and wrapped it up and placed

it on top of the deep freeze next to the paint can. He kneeled in front of his eight-year-old. "You have ketchup on your mouth."

Ambroise licked the sides of his mouth. Mmm! The flavor was soooo.... *No! Remember!* He had—

"*Please,* Dad?"

When an issue was referred to his father, Ambroise knew it probably wouldn't happen, but he had to try.

His father stood and put his arm around the dragon's shoulders. "Let's go."

They went upstairs. "Come on everybody!" the father hollered. "Let's go! Get your coats on, hats and gloves and boots—we're going to the park!"

Ben's mother gave a questioning look to her husband, who gave her a quick kiss.

Gui jumped up from the couch and clapped sharply. "Going to the park!" he yelled in an announcer's voice.

"Let's go, boys!" their father said. He patted the dog. "Ready, Mike?"

Mike wagged his thick tail and sneezed.

The Weimer family loaded into their van, all bundled up for a winter day. It was snowing even harder and normally Ben would have appealed to bring their sleds, but Ambroise resisted the urge, relieved that they were actually going. If only it weren't too late....

Ben and the Dragon

Chapter 12 – HAPPY

Viewing the Flushing pond in the inky reflective pool, Ben felt his old self rise to the surface of his mind, even though he was still a dragon. Crouched on the rock shore, he tried to remember the fun times he'd had at the park floating below. But like a foot that has fallen asleep, even though he wanted to remember, he couldn't.

And then—his memories bobbed to the surface like slow-rising bubbles. Sledding in a "train" last winter on the other side of the park, crashing and laughing in a pile of sleds and kids and snow. He remembered sliding down the spiral slide on the pond side of the park with Gui and Mom, and even Mike climbing the slide with

Dad's help and going down! He remembered counting the minnows in the water. He remembered everything.

Sadness accompanied these memories as he watched the empty pond scene. He knew he couldn't last another day. His cobalt blue dragon's eyes stared unblinking as he considered this. His long, toothed, lightly-scaled snout was dry and tearless.

In the pool scene below, it was snowing heavier. Background trees and the pond's edge were fuzzy and occasionally faded away before refocusing. *Probably the wind*, he thought, leaning closer. *Oh, no!*

Whiteness took over. Nothing more was visible. The connection was disappearing and he would be trapped in Diamant, like Ricard....

What?

Much larger in the scene than Ben would have expected, Mike was sniffing at the edge of the pond. The big white English Labrador lapped water with his front feet submerged, and then raised his head, drops

falling from his muzzle. He stared directly at Ben, a dragon leaning over the edge of the *l'eau* pool.

"Hi, Mike!" Ben rumbled loudly through chest slits.

The dog's wet nose wiggled as he sniffed.

Ben's long teeth were inches above the pool. He stared into the surface and tried to see past Mike. He strained, listening....

Mike backed away and padded off toward faint noises that Ben could hear approaching.

From the right, a running boy entered the scene wearing a familiar winter jacket. Was it? It *had* to be.

"Ambroise!" he rumbled in his loudest dragon voice. The black *l'eau* surface rippled with the sound.

He couldn't approach closer without touching the pool and risking severing the *Temps-rapproché* connection—or even worse, he might change places with a minnow! Ben held himself back, impatiently.

The sound of voices drew nearer.

"Ben!" his dad shouted.

"Ben, don't!" Gui yelled.

The dragon was unaccustomed to running on two legs, let alone while bundled up in winter clothing. When he reached the pond's edge, he saw beyond Mike a shadowy area of darkness...

Yes!

Ambroise stopped with his boots in the water. In the dark shadow, a familiar *visage* was reaching forward. His dragon self inside this boy's body felt a powerful rush of emotions. Tears ran down his cheeks. He was breathing hard. His heart was pounding.

"Ben!" he shouted in his boy's voice.

A dragon crouching by the *l'eau* pool in Diamant heard his own voice saying his own name.

"Yes!" he answered in his dragon rumble, "It's me!"

Ambroise was relieved to hear his own tones rumbling from the shadow image. "Lean closer, Ben," he said to the dragon. "We must touch our barriers at the same time!"

Rushing noises in the grass behind him almost made Ambroise jump. "Ready?" he yelled. The shadow dragon nodded. The boy stepped forward and reached into the water with an eager human hand.

"Now!"

On a far-away world, the dragon touched its crystal snout to the *l'eau* pool.

There was a bright flash. And then nothing. The dragon fell backwards—again.

§

"Ben!" his mother exclaimed, kneeling and cradling his head. "What are you doing?"

Ben laughed and laughed. He was overcome with joy and relief. He could feel every emotion that he couldn't feel when he was a dragon. He was on his back in the grass at the edge of the pond—*his* pond! He could feel his own body again. It was soooo good.

"Mom, Dad; I'm so glad! I'm so glad!" The boy hugged his mother and then his father, who was just kneeling, with all of his might.

His father looked over his son's head at a shadow in the water...

"I was a dragon, Dad! And now I'm back!"

Ben scrambled to his feet. "See?" He pointed to the dragon he saw floating in the water.

"Hi Ambroise!" he said.

The shadow dragon nodded. To his left stood the crimson *Gardien* Ricard.

"Farewell, Benjamin," Ambroise rumbled, sounding very far away. The shadow image faded. In a few seconds it was gone.

"I'll never forget you, Ambroise!" Ben yelled. He looked up at his father. He had never been *so* happy.

"Did you see him, Dad? I was in Diamant and he was here! That was Ambroise."

The father was frowning as he thought of two crystal blue eyes....

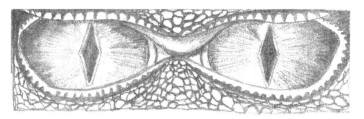

Eyes? He shook his head.

Ben's excited explaining continued. It was snowing harder.

"Come on, Ben," The boy's father was relieved that his younger son seemed back to normal. "Come on, everybody."

Benjamin, Guillaume, mother, father and Mike made their way uphill in the heavily falling snow. The boy continued telling his story about where he'd been during the past day and night.

Ben and the Dragon

Epilogue – Wayward Sons

The mother was relieved at her younger son's return to himself. His fixation on the fantastic tale of a crystal dragon world.... *This boy's going to be something one day*, she thought.

§

On his first night back, Ben dreamed of Diamant and flew once again with his *Gardien* friend, Ricard—and Ambroise was there, too! He told his dragon brother all about his time on Diamant and Ambroise told him about his adventures in Ben's life. The sleeping boy smiled.

His parents closed the bedroom door. "He seems okay," the father whispered.

§

Ben's parents waited several days before allowing him to return to the Flushing Park. When they did go, the whole family, Mike included, went down to the edge of the pond and looked for the dragon's shadow.

Nothing.

Ben *knew* that the close-time was over. A dragon's ability that remained in his mind from Ambroise's time there, the boy would *always* know what time it was and how much time had passed.

He never saw Ambroise again.

In the following years, Ben was never the same boy, young man or man that he might have been. A crystal dragon's world remained inside. A steady, calm dragon outlook stayed with him for the rest his life, which was a very long and exciting one.

What did all of this mean?

If you had asked Ben this question as a young man, he would have smiled and looked at you without saying anything. To the end of his days, he never again felt lonely or afraid of the dark; it had become his friend and comforter.

Always knowing that someone, out there, remembered him, perfectly, forever, was... *perfect.*

Breathing fire, flying, feasting on moonlight and knowing everything about the dragons—it was all etched into his mind like an eternal diamond. He never forgot a single detail. A dragon's memory was unchanging and permanent. He, the human, might not live forever, but in his own way, he had become an immortal dragon.

§

Light years away, circling its brilliant blue sun, a moonlit planet held a similar soul.

Ambroise never forgot living in Ben's family.

In the thousands of unblinking years that followed his off-world adventure, Ambroise experienced something which had been impossible for his kind before.

Whenever his thoughts returned to being a boy in his human family, the crystal dragon on a blue-shadowed world would land and settle by the *l'eau* pool, stare into the dark liquid, and for eternal moments

dream.

The End

I thank *my* family. I didn't have to invent anything; *Ben and the Dragon* is from our lives. Two brothers, a mother and father, a dog, the house we live in, our village pond, home painting projects—it all was only shuffled and arranged, never changed.

Ben, the real-life boy in this story, is a beacon of curiosity and joy. Thank you, son, for the Christmas of your eighth year that I could write this story for.

For those of you who helped me to make this book a reality, I say, *help is a snowflake*. Thank you.

Faith Lancaster, mother of Charlie, the real-life friend of my sons who appears in this story, thank you for proofreading this book twice.

Wyatt Wright, fellow wonderer and father to a younger son, thank you for reading and reacting to both early and late manuscript bookends.

Shawn Pethel, father of two sons, too, thank you for reading an early draft of *Ben and the Dragon* at bedtime to your boys, and sharing their reactions.

Finally, thank you **Andrée**, my artist wife, for putting up with my occasional moodiness during this work in progress. Illustrating *Ben and the Dragon* and painting its cover image are the icing on this cake. Thank you, sweetie.

CPSIA information can be obtained at www.ICGtesting.com
Printed in the USA
LVOW06s1235141013

356761LV00001B/1/P